One-Minute
Favorite
Fairy Tales

One-Minute Favorite Fairy Tales

by

Shari Lewis

Illustrated by Benton Mahan

DOUBLEDAY & COMPANY, INC.
GARDEN CITY, NEW YORK

TO ANN RITZ HURWITZ
"You may have tangible wealth untold;
Caskets of jewels and coffers of gold.
Richer than I you can never be—
I had a Mother who read to me."
—Strickland Gillilan

Me, too. Thanks, Mom.
—Shari Lewis

Library of Congress Cataloging in Publication Data

Lewis, Shari.
  One-minute favorite fairy tales.

  Summary: Twenty familiar fairy tales from many
countries, condensed so they may be read in just one
minute.
  1. Fairy tales. [1. Fairy tales. 2. Folklore]
I. Mahan, Ben, ill. II. Title.
PZ8.L481250n 1985 [398.2] [E] 84-25968
ISBN: 0-385-19322-X

Contents

One-Minute Favorite Fairy Tales

To the Parents

A TV talk-show host recently challenged me: "Why tell one-minute fairy tales?" I immediately responded, "That's a three-part question; which part would you like answered first?"

Startled, she said, "What are the three parts?"

Then it was my turn to be startled, because I had no idea where my mouth was taking me. However, I figured that my mouth had gotten me into this and I'd better trust it to get me out, so I let it roll and it went something like this.

I said, "The first question you've asked is 'Why tell *one-minute* stories, as opposed to longer ones?' Well, I'm certainly not opposed to longer stories. No home should be a one-story-book household. 'One-Minute Fairy Tales' is just another light-hearted alternative.

"After all, there are those nights when parents don't have the energy to read the full-length authorized biography of Tom Thumb—it's clearly a no-no for the parent telling the bedtime story to fall asleep before the child! Better to be truly involved with your youngster for a few minutes than to be only half there during those weary times when reading is not what you wish to be doing.

"One day, a five-year-old said to me, 'Mommy and Daddy work. They leave the house by Sesame Street and don't get home till Dan Rather.' That youngster summed up one of the most significant changes in contemporary parenting. Many folks in dual-income families are away all day. Those moms and dads know that they need to spend *quality* time with their kids since quantity is simply not available. One-minute stories fill this gap because they are excellent beginning points for communication and play.

"In my opinion, this is a good book to have around when your child protests, 'Just one more story!' And, of course, if you have more than a minute, you can always read more than one!

"Next, to answer part two of the question: 'Why tell *fairy* tales?'

"What do we pass on in these old stories? Glimpses of faraway lands. Attitudes of long-ago times. An example of good triumphing over evil, and honesty being rewarded. The greedy man being bested by the simple, generous and warm one. That all seems to be of value.

"Of course, in fairy tales, we also introduce a world in which violence was everywhere. But I feel that this apparent negative is more than balanced by the fact that kids experience these threats and injustices in the safety of their parents' laps. Parent and child can share that momentary fear. Psychologists tell us that learning to cope with make-believe fears is the first step toward coping with real ones. Basically, this feast of fairy tales serves up magic—whether the magic is mystical (telling of the 'wee folk,' giants and witches) or the magic of love ('happily ever after' tales involving princes and princesses from wonderful palaces—stories that never will be, and perhaps never were).

"And so fairy tales offer the same relief today that they have brought to people in other times and other places—an escape from the gravity of everyday life.

"Finally, in answer to the third question—'Why tell *tales* at all?'—nothing bridges that gap between daytime and night-time, between parent and child, as well as a story. These are rituals of sharing and communication.

"You needn't be an actor to be a successful storyteller. Just read the words.

"I've never met a child who wouldn't turn off the TV set for a real live lap and a real live story."

By this time, my TV talk-show host was wildly signaling me to "cut," so I did.

And although I have lots more to say on the subject, I'll now take my book editor's suggestion to stop, as well!

Love,

Shari Lewis

Sleeping Beauty
German

A long time ago, a Queen gave birth to her first child, a princess. Her husband, the King, was so overcome with joy he decided to hold a huge feast, and invited all his friends and relations. He wanted to invite the thirteen fairies of the kingdom, too, but since he had only twelve golden plates, one fairy had to stay home. Angered at being left out, the thirteenth fairy appeared before the King and Queen and declared, "When the princess is sixteen, she will prick her finger on a spinning wheel and die."

A good fairy, who was a friend of the King and Queen, could not undo the curse, but she could change it a little. She said, "Although the princess must prick her finger on that spinning wheel, she won't die. She will sleep for a hundred years and remain young until she awakens."

The baby princess grew to be a big, beautiful princess, but the nasty fairy's curse came true. At sixteen, the princess pricked her finger on a spinning wheel and fell into a deep, deep sleep.

A century later, a prince from a neighboring kingdom was riding by the castle, and saw the sleeping princess. She looked so peaceful that he kissed her, and (as happens in fairy tales) the evil spell was broken. Sleeping Beauty awakened, married the prince, and from what I hear, she never did tell him how old she really was.

Chit-Chat

African

One day, a farmer was in his field, getting ready to pull some sweet potatoes out of the ground in order to sell them at the market, when one of the sweet potatoes said, "Fine, now you want to pull me up and sell me, but all the time I've been growing, you've hardly given me any water."

Startled, the farmer looked around and said, "Who's talking to me?" And his dog replied, "It was the sweet potato, you silly farmer!"

The farmer had never heard of a talking sweet potato *or* a talking dog—and he became a bit frightened. To protect himself, he started to pull a big branch from a tree. "Oh, no, you don't," said the tree. "You can't take a branch from me to use as a stick. For years you've been enjoying my shade without ever saying 'Thank you.'"

Now the farmer was *really* frightened. And he ran all the way to the King's castle.

When he arrived, he told the King exactly what had happened. "First the sweet potato talked to me," he said, "then the dog, then the tree."

"I think," said the King, "you've been working in the sun too long. You need a rest." And he waved the farmer away.

After the farmer left, the King pulled up his favorite chair. As he did, the chair laughed and said to the King, "Can you believe that farmer? Who ever heard of a talking sweet potato?"

The Goose and the Golden Eggs

German

There was an old farmer in Kalamazoo
Who was starving and didn't know what to do—
Until a stranger arrived at the farm,
Carrying a goose under his arm.

"Take care of my goose," he said, "and friend,
The goose will take care of you, in the end."
And before the next day was an hour old,
The goose laid an egg that was made of gold.

All that week and the next, I'm told
The goose laid eggs that were made of gold.
The farmer sold the eggs, made lots of dough.
He became rich, but then, you know . . .
He said, "I really think it's a crime
To have to make money *one egg at a time.*
That silly old goose, she makes me sore!
I'll bet in her belly, she has dozens more!"

So the farmer grabbed it by the legs
And killed the goose with the golden eggs.
There were none inside the goose, of course,
Which filled the farmer with remorse.
Soon his money was gone, and he was needy.
See what you get for being greedy?

The Frog Prince

German

Of all the toys the princess had, she loved her golden ball the most. One day, the ball bounced into a deep dark well. The princess had just begun to cry when she heard a deep grumbly voice say, "If I get your ball back, will you promise me something?" She looked up to see a great, green, grinning frog.

The princess said she would promise him *anything* if he'd get her ball back. So the frog dove down, and quickly came back up with it.

"Well," the princess said, "what do you want me to promise?" "That you will let me live with you and be your friend," answered the frog. "I'll have to think about *that,*" the princess replied. She skipped back to the palace, and didn't think about it at all.

14

A week later there was a knock on her bedroom door. She opened it and there stood the frog and her father, the King.

"The frog told me of your promise to him," the King said. "A princess never breaks a promise." But the frog could see that the princess didn't want to be his friend. So, tearfully, he said good-bye.

"Wait," said the princess. "Don't be sad. I will be your friend." And, to prove it, she picked him up and kissed him.

Suddenly the frog was gone. In its place stood a fine prince who said, "Only the kiss of a kind-hearted princess could erase the curse that a witch had put on me."

And they became friends.

Soon, they were such good friends, that the only thing to do was to marry. So they did!

One Particular Small, Smart Boy

Persian

Once upon a time a little boy was walking home from the village with only an egg and some salt in his pocket. Suddenly a big, mean giant jumped out from behind a tree and said, "Say your prayers, little boy! I'm going to eat you up for lunch!"

The boy, who was small but very smart, quickly said, "Oh great Giant, I know you are strong, but so am I. Let's have a contest to see who's the strongest."

The giant snorted, "Compared to me, you're no bigger than a blade of grass. I'll mow you down right now. On with the contest!"

The boy quickly snuck the egg from his pocket into the palm of his hand where the giant couldn't see it. He picked up a rock in that same hand and said, "I challenge you to squeeze this rock until water comes out, as I will!" Then the boy squeezed the egg and the rock together until the eggshell broke and egg oozed between his fingers. Of course, the giant thought the water actually came from the rock, and he was shocked.

Then the boy secretly took some salt from his pocket, picked up another rock and said, "Now I'm going to squeeze this rock into salt." After a few squeezes, he let the salt pour out. Then he turned to the giant. "And now, give me your *hand* and I'll squeeze it into mud!"

But the giant cried, "Oh no, you won't!" and he ran away, never to bother that particular small, smart boy again.

Baba Yaga was a Russian witch who (it is said) used to wander the forest, looking for bad Russian children to eat for dinner. However, unless you are a bad Russian child don't give her a second thought.

Baba Yaga and the Hedgehog

Russian

Baba Yaga was searching for a black sunflower. She knew that if she ate its petals she would live for another two hundred years.

However, she found a hedgehog instead. Since she had no sunflower, Baba Yaga decided the hedgehog would do for dinner. And the next thing he knew, that hedgehog was in a pot surrounded by vegetables.

"Don't eat me, Baba Yaga," pleaded the little animal.

Baba Yaga was shocked. "Who taught you to speak so well?"

"As my mother and father were admiring a beautiful flower in their garden, Mother said, 'I wish I could have a son, even if he were no bigger than a hedgehog.' Soon after that, I was born. Everybody laughed at them because they had a hedgehog for a son, and so I was sent away to live in the forest.

18

Can you imagine? All because of a big black sunflower!"

Baba Yaga gasped, and quickly said, "Take me to that sunflower and I won't cook you for dinner."

And the hedgehog did.

The minute Baba Yaga pulled up that black sunflower by its roots, the hedgehog turned into a little boy named Ivan, who ran home to his mother and father.

And so Baba Yaga didn't eat the hedgehog, and she *did* eat the leaves of the black sunflower, and she *did* live for another two hundred years, but the time is up by now, so you *certainly* needn't worry!

Thumbelina

Danish

Thumbelina was born inside a beautiful tulip and even though she was no bigger than a thumb, she sure was cute! So cute, in fact, that one day a mean old frog, who happened to be hopping by, saw her, said, "You're going to marry my son," and carried her away.

Placing Thumbelina on a large green lily pad the frog went off to fetch her son. But as poor Thumbelina began to cry, a passing fish overheard her and pulled the lily pad across the river to the edge of the forest. Thanking the fish, Thumbelina quickly ran away as fast as she could.

Deep in the forest, she came upon a wounded bird, whom she nursed back to health. In order to repay her, the bird said,

20

"Climb on my back and I will take you to the most beautiful garden in the world."

When they arrived, inside one of the flowers was a transparent man. You could see right through him! He was no bigger than Thumbelina, and he was wearing a golden crown.

"I am the Spirit of the Flowers," said the man. "My friend, the bird, has told me of your kindness. And you're just my size! Would you like to be my wife?"

Thinking she'd probably be better off with this man than with a frog, Thumbelina said, "Yes." The little man led her to a throne which was in the flower right next to his, and there these two tiny people joyfully spent the rest of their days.

Scheherazade

Arabian

There was once a very powerful but cruel Arabian king, called a Sultan, who had several wives. When the Sultan tired of them, he decided to have them beheaded.

He said, "I'm going to kill one wife each day, but I can't do it myself. I'll have my assistant, the Grand Vizier, do it for me."

The Grand Vizier's daughter, Scheherazade, was horrified at the news. But the Vizier knew that if he refused, the Sultan would kill him, too. So Scheherazade said, "I'll give myself to the Sultan as his next bride, and I'll put an end to all of this nonsense!"

The Sultan was delighted to take Scheherazade as wife, but he assured the Grand Vizier that there would be no exceptions. The morning after the wedding, this wife would die, too.

Scheherazade and the Sultan were married, and that night

she started to tell him a wonderful story. By the Sultan's bedtime, the story had not endcd, so hc said he would let Scheherazade live an extra day, until she finished the talc. The next night she told more of her fabulous story, but once again, the Sultan's bedtime came before the story's end.

At this point, the Sultan was completely enchanted with the story, and was beginning to be enchanted by the clevcr girl, as well.

Scheherazade managed to make her story last for 1,001 nights. By then, the Sultan realized that he loved Scheherazade, and a vow to love is greater than a vow to kill. So she really became his wife, once and for all, which put an end to his wife-killing—but not to her storytelling!

The Fairies
French

There once was a widow who had two daughters. The older was like her mother—nasty, proud and unpleasant—and the younger took after her father and was very kind.

But the mother loved the nasty older daughter and made her sweet young daughter do all the work, including going to the well for water.

One day, a fairy disguised as a ragged woman came to the well and asked for a drink. The pleasant girl gave it to her gladly. The fairy said, "Since you are so kind, I shall make you a gift: Every time you speak a word, a jewel or flower will fall from your lips."

When the girl arrived home with her jug of water, she was scolded for being late. "Forgive me," said the poor girl, and a rose and a pearl fell from her mouth.

Stunned, her mother said, "What happened to you at the well?" As her daughter told her, diamonds, rubies and emeralds came tumbling out.

So the very next day, the mother sent her *older* daughter down to the well, thinking that she, too, would be charmed when she spoke. The older daughter went, grumbling all the way.

At the well, the ragged woman asked for a drink. The older sister snapped, "Here. Have your drink and hurry up."

"That's not very polite," said the ragged woman. "Since you're so nasty, I shall give you a gift: Each time you speak, a frog or a snake shall fall from your lips."

As the older daughter approached home, her mother ran out to meet her. "Well, how did it go?"

"Not so well, Mother," said the nasty girl, and two frogs and two snakes jumped from her mouth.

Then the fairy suddenly appeared before them in shimmering clothes. "Your sister's kindness was rewarded with diamonds and pearls; your nastiness, with frogs and snakes. In this life, you get what you give!"

The Doll in the Grass

Scandinavian

One day a great King said to his sons, "To share my kingdom, you must each go out and find a wife who can spin and weave and make a shirt, all in one day."

The next morning, when the brothers set out, they told the youngest brother, whose name was Ash Paddle, to go another way because he was so slow.

Ash Paddle was so sad that he began to cry. A voice, deep in the grass, said, "Why are you so unhappy?" Ash Paddle parted the grass and saw a tiny girl. He told her his sad story.

"I can spin and weave and make a shirt for you," she said. And quickly, she did. It was a very tiny shirt, but Ash Paddle loved it. "Will you be my wife?" he said.

"You don't mind the fact that I am so tiny?" she asked.

"I only care that you were kind to me," said Ash Paddle.

"Very well," she said, "but first, please take me to the lake."

Ash Paddle carried her to the lake, where she jumped into the water and disappeared.

Ash Paddle thought he had lost her forever and began to cry. His tears dropped onto the tiny shirt, which instantly grew to normal size. At that moment, the girl came out of the lake, fully grown!

"A witch placed a spell on me, but kindness can break any witch's spell," she said.

So they went back to the King, who liked this kind girl, too, and shared a part of his kingdom for all of their days.

27

Little Red Riding Hood

German

Red Riding Hood started to Grandma's
With cider, fruit and cake.
In the woods she met the Wolf
Who was hiding near a lake.

Red Riding Hood saw the Wolf
But didn't shrink back in alarm
When he said, "Where are you going
With that basket under your arm?"

"I'm going to my Grandma's house
With cider for her thirst—
And some cake—"
She stopped.
The Wolf was gone.
The Wolf got to Grandma's first.

The Wolf threw Grandma in the closet,
Then hopped into her bed.
When Little Red got to Grandma's
The Wolf was there, instead.

The Wolf was dressed in Grandma's clothes,
Her nightgown and her wig.
"Oh, Grandma," said Red Riding Hood,
"Your ears are very big."

"The better to hear you," said the Wolf,
"The better to hear you laugh."
"Your nose has grown," said Riding Hood,
"It's bigger, by more than half."

"The better to smell you with," said the Wolf
With a gruesome grin.
"My mouth is larger too, and now
I'm going to pop you in!"

Then with a shout, he showed his teeth
And jumped up out of bed.
But nearby, a hunter heard
And that hunter shot him dead!

Rapunzel

German

Once there was a beautiful maiden named Rapunzel, who had the longest hair in the world. Brought up by a jealous old witch, she lived all alone in a room atop a tall tower, deep in the woods. Whenever the witch wanted to talk to Rapunzel, she would call, "Rapunzel, Rapunzel, let down your long hair." Rapunzel would then lower her long braid from the window and the witch would climb up the braid.

One day a prince was riding by the tower, and he saw the witch climb the braid to the top of the tower. As soon as the witch left, he called, "Rapunzel, Rapunzel, let down your long hair." Rapunzel lowered her long braid and the prince climbed up to Ra-

punzel's room. They soon became great friends, and the prince promised to return again.

Unfortunately, the witch was watching in her crystal ball and she became furious. She cut off Rapunzel's long braid, nailed one end of it to the windowsill, and dangled the braid out of the window. Then she banished Rapunzel to live in a little house, far, far from anywhere.

When the prince returned (as he had promised) and climbed up the braid of hair, instead of Rapunzel he found the wicked witch, who cursed him and took away his eyesight.

The poor blind prince wandered the earth for many years, but one day he chanced upon a little house far, far from anywhere. And there was Rapunzel. She recognized him, and, crying with happiness, threw her arms around him.

Her tears fell on his eyes and broke the evil curse. He rubbed his eyes and saw her too, and their friendship flourished forever and forever.

The Flying Horse

Persian

Once there was a ninety-year-old magician who possessed a magical wooden horse. But the man was lonely, and wanted a wife to share his life with. He proposed a trade to the King: The wooden horse for the King's daughter's hand in marriage.

"The horse has two pins," the magician said to the King. "When one is twisted the horse will fly wherever you wish. The other pin, when twisted, will bring the horse home again."

The King was so delighted that he promised the magician he could marry his daughter.

When the princess saw that her husband-to-be was ninety years old, she ran crying to her brother, who begged his father to take back his promise.

The magician overheard the brother's plea. "I must get rid

of this meddling young man!" he decided. He approached the brother, and showing him the handsome horse said, "Look what I have brought as a gift for your father."

Of course, when the prince heard that the wooden horse could fly, he wanted to try it out. He leapt into the saddle, twisted the pin to which the magician had pointed, and the horse immediately rose into the air.

But the magician had not told the prince of the other pin, which would bring the horse home again. And so the prince was never heard from again. But neither was the magic horse. Unable to complete his trade with the King, the old magician couldn't marry the princess after all!

33

The Cat of Catton

Swedish

Once a brother and sister had to share what was left when their parents died. They both wanted the cow. Neither wanted the cat.

The cat purred to the sister, "Please take me, I promise we'll both have a happy ending." So she did.

Traveling through the forest they came upon a castle. The cat said, "Little sister, hide your ragged clothes under this bush." Then he scampered up to the castle and began to wail, "A princess from another kingdom has been robbed. She's lost absolutely everything!"

The Queen and her son, the prince, upset that such a terrible thing happened to a princess, sent new clothes and invited her in. She was a sweet girl, and she looked nice in her new clothes. The prince admired her kindness, and after a while he asked this "princess" to be his wife.

34

But the Queen didn't believe that the girl was a real princess. She asked, "Where is your kingdom?" The cat whispered to the girl, "Say you come from the Land of Catton." She did, but the Queen was still suspicious.

As a test, under a bed made of piles of pillows, the Queen put a bean. "A real princess, used to comfort, will feel this bean," thought the Queen. But the cat was watching and told the girl.

In the morning, the girl said, "Thank you for the pillows, but I felt as though there was a rock under my bed."

Then the Queen placed a blade of grass under many mattresses, but again the cat was watching.

That second morning, the girl said, "I felt as though there was a wooden beam under the mattresses."

That convinced the Queen that this girl was really, truly the Princess of Catton, and the Queen gave her blessings. The princess married the prince. The cat had the run of the castle for years and years, and all had a happy ending, just as the cat had promised!

The Porridge Pot

German

Once upon a time a poor little girl lived with her poor mother in a town that was so poor that people had hardly anything to eat.

One day the poor little girl was on the road begging for food when she met a generous old woman who pitied her and gave her a little iron pot.

"You need only say to it, 'Little Pot Boil!'" said the old woman, "and it will boil sweet porridge for you. Then say, 'Little Pot Stop' and it will stop boiling."

Thanking the old woman, the little girl took the pot home and said, "Little Pot Boil!" The pot immediately boiled enough porridge to last for days.

"Little Pot Stop!" she cried . . . and immediately the pot stopped boiling.

A few weeks later, while the little girl was away, visiting a friend, her mother became hungry. "Little Pot Boil!" she said.

The pot obediently began boiling porridge. But the poor lady hadn't heard that she had to command the pot to *stop* boiling, and so after a while it boiled over. The porridge bubbled onto the kitchen floor, it slopped out the door, it rolled down the streets and into everyone's house.

As she walked home, the little girl saw the great river of porridge. She cried out, "Little Pot Stop!" Of course it did!

Well, all the townspeople had to eat their way back into their houses, but no one complained, for they weren't hungry again for months.

37

Twelve Dancing Daughters

German

A great King once had twelve daughters who slept together in one room, which was locked each night when they went to bed. Yet each morning the King was amazed to find that the princesses' satin shoes had been worn to pieces during the night. The King offered half his kingdom to anyone who could find out how his daughters wore out their shoes each night.

After meeting with the King, a clever young soldier followed them to their room one evening. He was wearing a magic cloak, one that made him invisible, and so he discovered that when the oldest princess jumped up and down on her bed three times, it sank into the ground, revealing a staircase.

The soldier followed the princesses down the stairs and through a wood to an enchanted castle where twelve princes awaited. He watched as the princesses and princes drank from large golden goblets. Then they danced and danced until their shoes were worn through. They danced until morning came, and the cock crowed.

The soldier took one of the golden goblets back to the King and told him what he had seen. The King kept his promise and gave the soldier half his kingdom, and gave his daughters a new bedroom at the other end of the castle, where there were no trapdoors!

The Nightingale and the Hawk

Origin unknown; attributed to Aesop

Sitting in its nest on the branch of an old oak tree was a nightingale singing a beautiful song. Suddenly, a big hawk swooped down, caught the little bird in its sharp claws, and swiftly carried it away.

"What are you going to do with me?" asked the nightingale. "I can see there's no chance of your letting me go. I know I wouldn't, if I were you."

The hawk was shocked. "Are you saying that if you were me, you'd eat yourself for supper? Is this some kind of a trick?"

The nightingale shrugged. "No. You are quick and strong. I am small and weak. You control the skies. I only share a few

40

trees with the squirrels and all of their walnuts."

"Walnuts?" said the hawk. "You know where the squirrels keep their walnuts?"

"Of course," said the nightingale. "I go there all the time."

"I love walnuts," said the hawk. "I'll tell you what. If I let you go back to your branch, will you sing every time the squirrels' houses are full of walnuts? Then I could swoop down and gobble them up."

"Well, you drive a hard bargain," the nightingale said, "but . . . all right. It's a deal."

The hawk let the little bird go and watched him as he flew back to the old oak tree. So, whenever you hear the song of a nightingale, look out for a hungry hawk. He probably won't be far away.

The King, the Coin and the Clown

Arabian

The King's clown had always made him laugh. So when the
clown died, the King was very sad. One day, Stamboola, a
clown from another kingdom, heard about the sad King, and
said to him, "Sire, I will make you laugh again."

"But your silly stunts will remind me of my old clown, and
that will only make me sadder," said the King.

Stamboola smiled. "At least let me try." Then Stamboola
stood on his head and spoke. As he did, his words came tumbling out upside down.

But the King didn't laugh.

"*My* jester used to do that," said the King. "But I will give
you something for trying." And the King handed Stamboola a
bag full of a thousand royal coins. One coin slipped out of the

bag and rolled on the floor. Stamboola quickly picked it up.

The King said, "You're a greedy clown! I gave you a thousand coins, yet *one* is so important you had to pick it up!"

"I didn't pick it up because I was greedy," said Stamboola, "but because your face is on both sides of this coin. I couldn't just leave it there knowing that, on one side, your face was in the dirt, and on the other, your face could be stepped on by the Queen."

The King laughed at the clown's clever answer and said, "Stay with me, Stamboola. You have just made me laugh without thinking of my old clown."

So Stamboola kept the King rolling with laughter, and the King kept the clown rolling in coins!

The Sky Is Falling

English

One day, as Henny Penny was taking a walk, an acorn fell on her head.

"Oh my, I think the sky is falling," she said. "That could be dangerous. I'd better tell the King."

She hadn't gone far when she met Chicken Little.

"A piece of the sky has fallen on my head," clucked Henny Penny. "I'm going to see the King."

"I'll come with you," peeped Chicken Little, and rushed along with her. In a few

44

minutes they met Ducky Lucky.

"The sky is falling!" cried Henny Penny. "We're going to see the King."

"Wait for me!" quacked Ducky Lucky.

At the edge of the woods the three met Foxy Loxy, and once again Henny Penny exclaimed, "The sky is falling! Want to come with us and tell the King?"

"Certainly," smiled Foxy Loxy, who knew better. "Sounds important."

And that's how sly old Foxy Loxy got to eat Ducky Lucky and Chicken Little. Henny Penny realized what was happening to her friends, but she firmly turned her head away, and pretended that she didn't see.

"The sky is falling," she said to herself, "I *must* see the King."

Poor Henny Penny, she wasn't able to recognize the real danger. Do I have to tell you what happened to her? In the end, she never *did* get to see the King!

Snow White and the Seven Dwarfs

German

Poor Snow White! Her stepmother was an evil Queen, who became insanely jealous every time the magic mirror said, "Snow White is prettier than you!" Finally she told the royal huntsman to take Snow White into the deepest part of the forest and kill her.

But the huntsman took pity on her, and, once in the forest, he told Snow White to run away.

Wandering through the forest, lost, tired and hungry, Snow White came upon a little cottage. Since no one was home, she went inside, ate some food, then lay down and took a nap.

The cottage belonged to seven dwarfs who worked in the

mines, deep in the mountains. When the little men came home, they found Snow White, fast asleep. She awakened and told them what had happened. They asked her to stay with them. She said yes.

Meanwhile, the Queen's mirror told her Snow White was still alive, at the dwarfs' cottage. The angry Queen dipped an apple in poison, dressed so that she looked like an old peddler and went to the cottage. She tricked Snow White into taking a bite. Poisoned, the girl fell into a very deep sleep.

The dwarfs, thinking she was dead, placed Snow White in a glass coffin.

A prince riding by saw Snow White, and was struck by her beauty. He kissed her, and she awakened. Soon, they became enchanted with each other and knew that their love would form a perfect circle which the wicked stepmother could never break to harm Snow White again. And do you know what? They were right!

World-famous ventriloquist and puppeteer **Shari Lewis** (also known as Lamb Chop's mother) has been honored with five Emmy awards, a Peabody, the Monte Carlo TV Award for World's Best Variety Show, and the 1983 Kennedy Center Award for Excellence and Creativity in the Arts, among others. One of the few female symphony conductors, she has performed with and conducted more than fifty symphony orchestras, throughout the United States and Canada, including the National Symphony at Kennedy Center and the National Arts Centre Orchestra of Canada.

Shari's previous book for Doubleday, *One-Minute Bedtime Stories,* is a juvenile bestseller and has been made into a home videocassette by Worldvision Enterprises. Also available is the "Shari Lewis Home Entertainment Library," recently released by MGM/UA, which includes three hour-long shows: *Have I Got a Story For You!, You Can Do It,* and *Kooky Classics.*

The author of twenty-six books, Shari is presently chairman of the board of trustees of the International Reading Foundation and has served on the national board of the Girl Scouts of the U.S.A. She is married to book publisher Jeremy Tarcher; their daughter, Mallory, recently graduated from Columbia University and works in the publishing industry.

Benton Mahan has illustrated many children's books. After graduating from the Columbus College of Art and Design in Columbus, Ohio, he moved to New York City, where he taught art at the Fashion Institute of Technology and worked as an illustrator. He currently lives in Ohio, near the farm where he grew up, and teaches part-time at the Columbus College of Art and Design. Mr. Mahan is married, has two daughters, and likes to travel and collect antiques.

48